D1028908

DECEMBER 13TH

Copyright © 2018 Christopher Butcher
All rights reserved
First Edition

PAGE PUBLISHING, INC.
New York, NY

First originally published by Page Publishing, Inc. 2018

ISBN 978-1-64138-341-7 (Hardcover)
ISBN 978-1-64138-340-0 (Digital)

Printed in the United States of America

DECEMBER 13TH

(A SHORT NARRATIVE)

Christopher Butcher

On December 13, I woke from my sleep. I hopped out of bed and on to my feet.

I'm searching the fridge for something to eat, when motion occurs a crick and a creek. I look to my right and nobody's there. A crick to my left, and now I'm aware.

4

5

I feel like a tortoise and slowly I stare in anger.
I shouted it better be hare.

Under the counter, I look for a sign. A snickering voice says, "Surely he's blind."

I turn back around and knock over rice then say to myself it may be the mice.

But nothing was quiet, and they weren't blind, and if it was rabbits, they're one of a kind. I looked at the tree. The presents were fine.

And if it's the Grinch, you're wasting your time. A snickering voice says, "Give him an *S*." The *S* could stand for nothing but stress. It would be so easy to give you the rest.

I say to myself, "Is this just a test?" I look for a ghost I may be the scrooge.

But I love Christmas, so now I'm a stooge. I'm searching the table for symbols and clues when somebody shouted it may be a rouge. If it is puck, you're all out of luck. If it is jack, you better get back. I know all you joker's tricksters and such, so step in the light or you're getting plucked.

The voices said, "Need feathers for that, and if we're a hit, you might need a bat. We'll give you a letter to keep you on track. The answer you need should be on your hat."

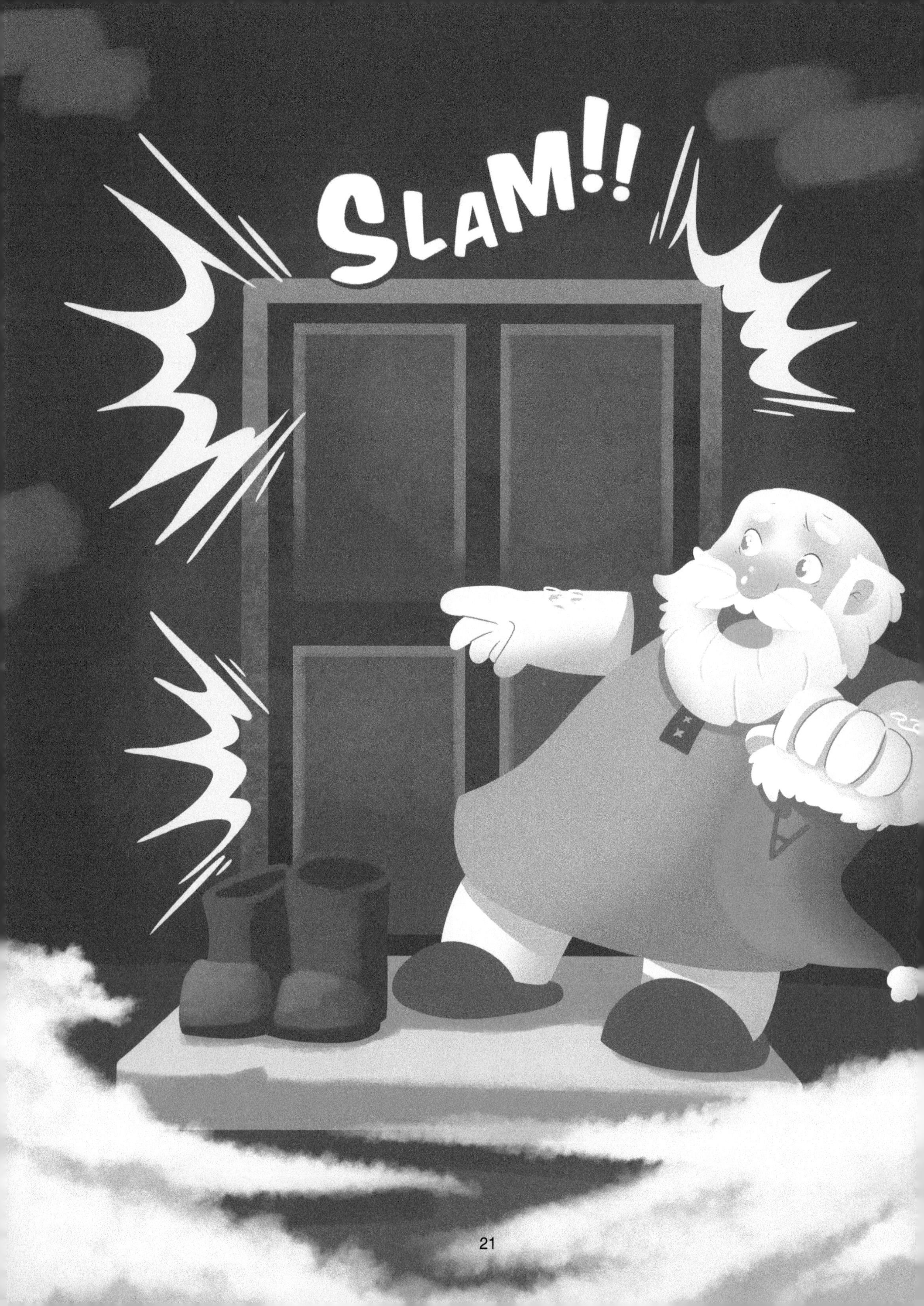
SLAM!!

I looked at the hat. The answer was *A* and guessing these letters was taking all day. It wouldn't take long if you would just play, so open the door, and we're on our way.

I opened the door, and boots were there. If this was a test, I wasn't prepared. I moved even closer to check out the air. When somebody shouted, I'm taking the dare. The door slammed shut and hit on my back.

I picked up the boots from off of the mat. I rammed through the door and tripped on the hat.

The voices said, "Did I do that?" The snickering voice turned into a laugh. "Get this one right and you're a giraffe. It would be so easy if you do the math. The answer you need should be in your path." I look at my path, and the answer was clear. They said that an *N* would keep me in gear.

They sound so tricky but also sincere. I looked at the fridge and a glass appeared. I put the glasses in front of my eyes.

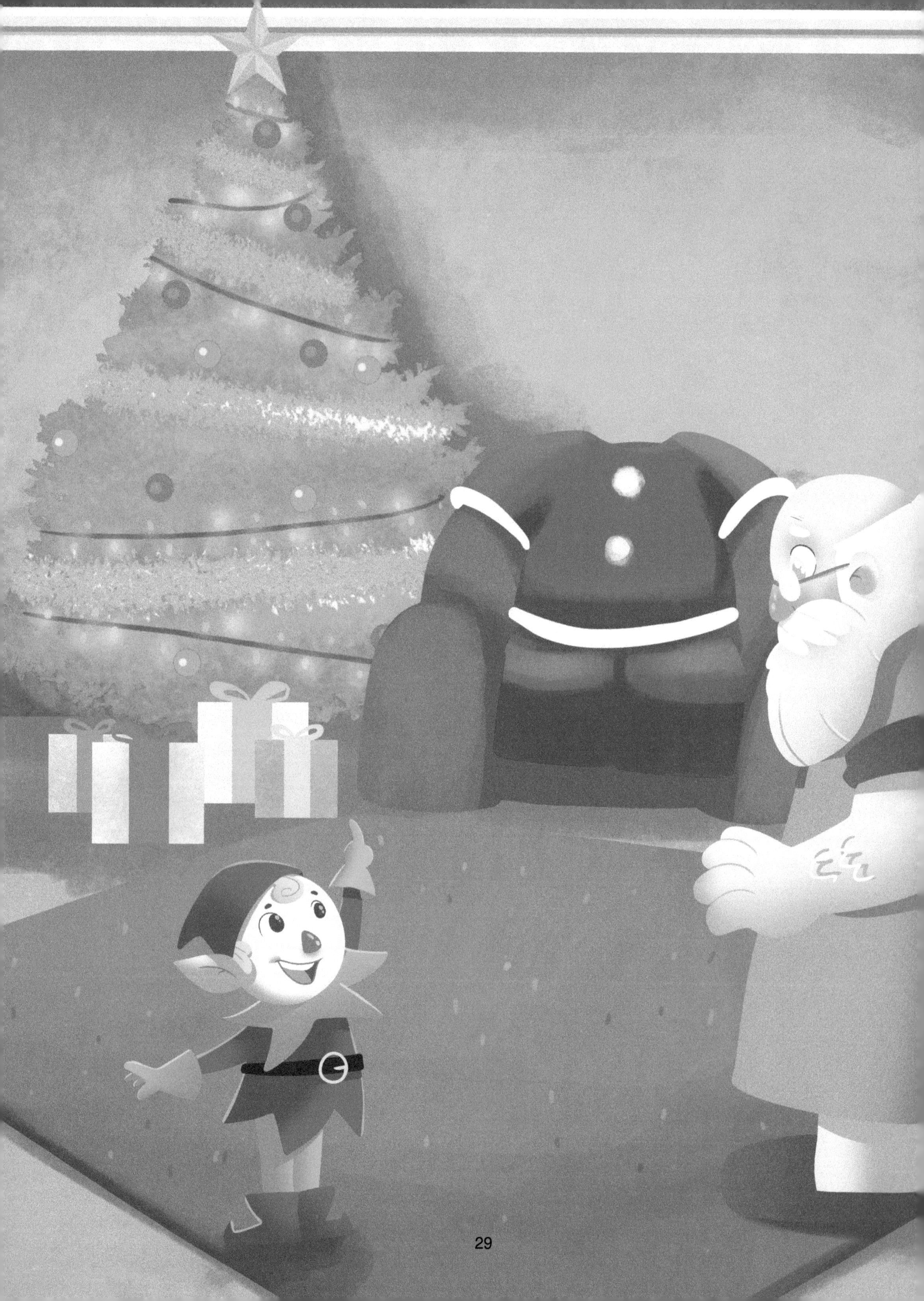

"For getting this far, we'll give you a prize."
I'm done with joking riddles and lies. I think
he means business. "We're half of your size."
One appeared and gave me a scare. If this was
a test, it hardly seems fair. It probably would if
you would compare what's up the tree to things
that you wear. A suit was there. The color was
red.

"We'll give you *T* since you are ahead." You said you would leave but giggle instead in anger.

I shouted, "You midgets are dead."

The midget appeared and said, "It's a wrap, so turn back around and pick up your hat and do not forget what you got off the mat, and grabbing the suit was part of your pack."

I picked up the hat and all I can see was *S-A-N* and also a *T*. The midgets were elves, so what could it be?

The answer was clear that Santa was me.

About the Author

Chris Butcher grew up in Baltimore, Maryland, with hopes of becoming famous. He has four brothers and two sisters. He is the middle child, and he believes he holds all of them together. Growing up in the streets of Baltimore was very difficult, especially being surrounded by so much negative energy. Even though he was still in school, he could feel the darkness following him as he age. One day, he came home from middle school and his uncle were in the basement rapping, and the rhythm sounded good to his ears and the base felt familiar to his body. So on that day, he decided he wanted to become a rapper. Years passed and he developed lot of skills that he thought would be his meal ticket, but none of them made him feel complete, like writing children's stories. *December 13th* is a very good story. Hope you enjoy reading it as much as Chris enjoyed writing it.